MAGGIE SPARKS

Published by Sweet Cherry Publishing Limited
Unit 36, Vulcan House,
Vulcan Road,
Leicester, LE5 3EF
United Kingdom

First published in the UK in 2022
2022 edition

2 4 6 8 10 9 7 5 3 1

ISBN: 978-1-78226-714-0

Maggie Sparks and the Swimming Pool Sharks

Cover design by Esther Hernando and Brandon Mattless
Illustrations by Esther Hernando

www.sweetcherrypublishing.com

Printed and bound in the United Kingdom
E.C007

MAGGIE SPARKS

AND THE
SWIMMING POOL SHARKS

STEVE SMALLMAN

ILLUSTRATED BY
ESTHER HERNANDO

Sweet Cherry

MAGGIE
That's me!

BAT
The coolest chameleon EVER.

MUM
Super smart.
Bakes great cookies.

DAD
Writes a lot.
Cannot bake cookies.

ALFIE
Stinky and
<u>annoying.</u>

GRANDAD
My favourite
wizard in the world!

AUNT CELIA
Posh. Likes weird food.

ELLA
World's worst
cousin!

ARTHUR
My best friend.

CHAPTER 1

Maggie Sparks was a witch. A small, curly-haired, freckle-faced witch, who was usually full of mischief and fizzing with

MAGIC.

But not today. Today she was mostly soggy.

She was walking through the park with her best friend, Arthur and it was raining … again. Maggie didn't like the rain. She didn't like the grey sky or the cold wind and she definitely didn't like the squelching sound the grass made when she walked on it. She thought it sounded like a frog being sick.

Arthur's older brother, Charlie, was supposed to be looking after them, but he had left them at the swings and hurried off to meet his *girlfriend* by the skateboard ramps, past the trees. Maggie looked around at the playground.

The swings were WET, the monkey bars were DRIPPING and the slide was SLIMY.

'Urgh, why does it have to rain all the time?' moaned Maggie. 'It's SOOOOOO boring! No wonder Bat decided to stay at home.'

'Actually,' said Arthur, 'rain is very important.'

'Why?' asked Maggie.

'It stops kingfishers getting tummy aches,' said Arthur.

'What *are* you talking about?' said Maggie.

'Well,' Arthur went on, 'if there wasn't any rain, all the streams and rivers would dry up. Then the fish would have nowhere to live, so they would die. And the dead fish would lie there in the sun and they would go all stinky and green.

But the kingfisher birds would still
eat them because they don't like pizza
or anything else. Then they would all
get tummy aches. So that's why rain is
very important.'

'No, it's not!' snapped Maggie,
kicking at a puddle. 'Why can't we
have snow instead?'

Maggie stopped walking as an idea
popped into her head.

'Maybe we *could* have snow,'
she said. 'With just a little bit of
MAGIC!'

'Oh dear,' sighed Arthur.

Maggie looked around. Apart from
a few damp ducks, the park was empty.

She gave her magic wand a wiggle
and chanted:

Magic spark
and magic fizzle,
bring us snow
instead of drizzle!

POOF!

The rain stopped and everything turned white.

'Wow,' said Arthur.

'**YES!**' shouted Maggie, punching the air. 'It worked! Grandad Sparks said that weather spells are *much* too

difficult for little witches. But I did it!
I actually did it!'

Maggie slid across the ice on the
newly frozen puddles. She made
snow angels on the grass and ran
around with her tongue sticking out,
trying to catch snowflakes.

Arthur, meanwhile, was building a
strangely familiar-looking snowman.

Then ... SPLOOF. A big fluffy white snowball hit Arthur on the back of his head and knocked him face down into the snow.

'Got you!' giggled Maggie.

Arthur picked himself up, wiped the snow from his glasses and put them back on. 'Hey, look!' he said. 'The fountain has frozen over.'

Maggie's eyes lit up.

'Let's skate on it,' she said, climbing over the low wall and stepping onto the ice.

'Be careful,' said Arthur, 'the ice might not be very thick.'

Maggie took no notice and was soon whizzing around the fountain like an Olympic ice-skating champion. Well, a wobbly Olympic ice-skating champion, in spotty wellies.

Maggie was having a lovely time, but her feet were getting very cold. 'Time for a little welly-warming MAGIC,' she said.

Maggie took out her wand,
gave it a wiggle and chanted:

Welly-warming
magic heat,
thaw my little
frozen feet!

POOF!

Maggie's toes started to tingle as her wellies grew warmer. 'That's better,' she sighed. She skated round the fountain, even faster than before. But the ice seemed to be getting more slippery at every turn.

'Maggie!' cried Arthur. 'I think you should stop skating now.'

'Why?' asked Maggie, whizzing past him.

'Your wellies are melting–'

'No, they're not, Arthur,' said Maggie. 'They're just warm.'

'No,' Arthur tried again. 'They're melting the ice!'

Maggie stopped, looked down and

... SPLASH!

She fell through the ice and into the freezing cold water.

CHAPTER 2

'Arthur, help!' screamed Maggie, thrashing her arms about. 'I CAN'T SWIM!'

'Try standing up,' said Arthur.

'HEEEELP MEEEEE! I CAAAAAAAAAAN'T SWIIIIIIIIM!'

Maggie cried even louder.

'STAND UP!' shouted Arthur.

Maggie stood up. The water only came up to the top of her wellies. She waded over to the edge of the fountain and Arthur helped her out.

Maggie's magic was wearing off now. The snow had started to melt and it was raining again.

A confused-looking Charlie walked back over. He saw the soggy state of Maggie and muttered, 'We're in so much trouble.'

'Oh, Maggie!' gasped Mum, as a sorry, soggy little witch squelched through the door. 'What happened to you? And where's Charlie?'

'Well …' Maggie began. She was trying to work out what to say to her mum that would get her in the least amount of trouble.

'Charlie's waiting outside – he didn't want to get in trouble. He only turned his back on us for a few minutes. But Maggie fell into the fountain,' said Arthur.

Maggie stared wide-eyed at Arthur, afraid that he might mention the 'm' word. She was not allowed to do magic on her own. And she was *definitely* not allowed to do weather spells.

'She was scared because she can't swim,' Arthur went on, 'and she was splashing around and shouting "HEEELP ME, ARTHUR! I CAAAAAAAAAN'T SWIM!". So I helped her out.'

'My poor darling,' said Mum,
wrapping Maggie up in a warm
towel. 'Thank you, Arthur. You can
go home now. I'll call your mum
and let her know what a brave boy
you are!'

'OK,' said Arthur, smiling broadly
as he stepped out of the front door,
towards a worried-looking Charlie.

Mum scooped Maggie up in her arms and ran a hot bath to warm her up. Then Mum found Maggie's warmest pyjamas, wrapped her up in a blanket on the sofa and brought her hot chocolate and cookies.

'This is great,' Maggie whispered
to Bat, her pet chameleon, who had
climbed onto her shoulder to check
that she was alright. Bat licked her ear
and turned a warm yellow colour (he
always did when Maggie was happy).

Mum sat down next to Maggie
and held her hand. 'You must have
been so scared,' she said.

'Oh, I was!' said Maggie.

'Especially because you can't swim,' said Mum.

'No, I can't,' said Maggie. 'Not even a little bit.'

Mum nodded, then stood up and walked out of the room.

A few minutes later, Mum came back in with a big smile on her face. 'Good news, Maggie,' she said. 'You don't have to worry about not being able to swim anymore.'

'Why?' asked Maggie.

'Because,' said Mum, 'I've booked you in for swimming lessons!'

OH NO!

CHAPTER 3

'Maggie?' said Mum. 'Are you ready? Your swimming lesson starts soon.'

Maggie stomped grumpily out of the changing cubicle.

'Oh, Maggie, you look ... GREAT!' said Mum, hiding a smile.

Maggie was wearing the new swimming costume Dad had bought for her. It was covered in little yellow ducks. Perched on top of her head was

a white swimming hat with a large
yellow duck in the middle that made
it look like a fried egg.

'I LOOK STUPID!'
said Maggie.

'Nonsense,' said Mum. 'You look very sweet.'

Maggie sighed as she looked down at the dozens of little ducks covering her tummy.

Bat wasn't helping. He was hidden inside Maggie's towel and was laughing so much that it shook.

They splashed through the foot bath and into the swimming pool area, where a tall, loud lady with a big smile and an even bigger hairdo was waiting to greet them.

She was wearing a bright green polo shirt and had a silver dolphin-shaped whistle hanging on a chain around her neck.

It was Mrs Flotsam, the swimming teacher.

'Oh, hello my dears,' she said in a silly sing-song voice, waving at them even though she was only a few steps away. 'And who's this little poppet in the adorable ducky swimsuit?' she asked.

Maggie glared at Mrs Flotsam, clenched her fists and said nothing.

'This is Maggie,' said Mum. 'It's her first lesson.'

'Wonderful!' said Mrs Flotsam. 'Well don't you worry, *Ducky*, we'll soon have you swimming like a little fishy.'

Bat had turned bright red because Maggie was feeling really grumpy now. She was NOT a "little poppet", her swimsuit was NOT "adorable" and her name was NOT "Ducky".

Maggie opened her mouth to speak, when someone popped out from behind Mrs Flotsam.

It was Arthur. He was wearing oversized swimming shorts, a T-shirt and goggles.

'What are *you* doing here?' asked Maggie.

'I'm supposed to be learning to swim,' said Arthur, miserably. 'But I've been coming for ages and I'm still only a Tadpole.'

'A what?' said Maggie.

'A Tadpole,' said Arthur. 'The beginners are called Tadpoles, then it's Ducklings, then Guppies, then Turtles, then Dolphins, then Sharks.'

'Well, I'll probably be a Shark then,' said Maggie, hopefully.

'No,' said Arthur. 'Hardly anyone gets to be a Shark because you have to swim a really long way and float on your back, and do different strokes, and dive in, and swim underwater in your pyjamas, and do handstands, and everything!'

'Who on earth could do all that?' asked Maggie.

'ME, ACTUALLY!' said a voice that Maggie knew only too well. It was her cousin, Ella.

Could this day get any worse? thought Maggie, turning around with a fake smile on her face.

Ella did **NOT** have a duck-infested swimsuit or a hat like an exploding boiled egg. She was wearing a smart navy-blue costume, covered in swimming award badges. Her hair was tucked neatly into her swimming hat and her brown eyes shone nearly as much as her dazzling smile.

She looked perfect. It was **SOOOOOOOOO** annoying!

Ella's mum, Aunt Celia, was
standing behind her.

'Hetty, darling!' she cried,
leaning over and kissing the air
next to Mum's ear.
'Fancy meeting
you here.'

Then she looked down at Maggie and said, 'Hello dear, what an *unusual* swimming costume.'

Maggie was about to reply when Mrs Flotsam blew her dolphin whistle and shouted, 'Into your groups, everybody!'

Arthur shuffled over to the Tadpole section, while Ella headed off to the Sharks. Maggie decided that she would rather be a Shark than a Tadpole, so she followed Ella.

'Oh no, Maggie, dear,' said Mrs
Flotsam so that everyone could
hear. 'You're not a Shark. You're
a TADPOLE!'

Maggie's cheeks grew very
pink as she stomped back to
the other side of the pool, with
Ella's pretty tinkling laugh
ringing in her ears.

Apart from Maggie
and Arthur, all the
other Tadpoles were
about three years
old. Yet Mrs Flotsam
talked to them all in
the same way.

'Come along my little Tadpoles, let's wiggle our way to the water. WIGGLE, WIGGLE, WIGGLE.

Are you WIGGLING, Maggie? No?
Well, never mind. Now let's climb
down the steps with a one, two,
three. Into the water, just like me!'

It took a long while before they were all standing in the water.

'When are we going to learn to swim?' Maggie asked Arthur.

'Not yet,' said Arthur, looking sadly at Mrs Flotsam, as if he knew what was about to come.

'Oh dear,' said Mrs Flotsam. 'I can
see some Tadpoles with dirty faces.
Let's all scoop up some water
and wash our faces.'

Everyone except
Maggie scooped up
water and washed
their face.

Maggie didn't like washing her face at home, so why would she do it here with pongy pool water?

'Well done, everybody!' said Mrs Flotsam. 'Well, *almost* everybody!' she added, looking straight at Maggie.

'Now we're all going to be little washing machines. Follow me.' Mrs Flotsam started waving her arms in circles like a startled seagull.

All the little children happily joined in. Arthur and Maggie joined in too, but not quite so happily.

Arthur didn't like to get water on his
goggles and Maggie was sure that Mrs
Flotsam was splashing them both
on purpose.

Then they all had to climb back out
of the pool, sit on the side with their
legs in the water and kick their feet.

'Come on everyone, get those little tootsies moving!' shouted Mrs Flotsam.

Maggie had had enough. When Mrs Flotsam turned away to deal

with a little boy who was kicking his sister instead of the water, Maggie took her chance. She pulled her wand out from under her swimming cap, gave it a wiggle and whispered:

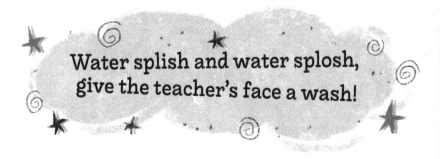

Water splish and water splosh, give the teacher's face a wash!

POOF!

All the water that the Tadpoles
were splashing up twirled into the
air like a mini tornado.

WHOOOOOO

OOSH!

It hit Mrs Flotsam like a tidal wave!

Maggie grinned and tucked her wand back into her cap.

Mrs Flotsam picked herself up. When she'd finished spluttering and coughing, she said, 'Good splashing, everybody! I think that's enough for today. See you all next week!'

All the mums came over to
collect their children as Mrs Flotsam
staggered off to the changing rooms
to get her towel.

'How did it go, Maggie? Did you
enjoy it?' asked Mum.

'I enjoyed the last bit,' said
Maggie with a sweet smile.

Her smile quickly faded when she heard Aunt Celia shout from across the pool. 'Hetty, Maggie, wait a minute!' She sped towards them with Ella in tow.

'Ella is a little tired because she just swam thirty lengths of the pool in a new club-record time. But she's *desperate* to know how Maggie's first lesson went.'

'Oh,' said Mum, 'that's very kind of you, Ella. It went very well, thank you.'

Ella leant a little closer to Maggie and whispered, 'Did you get your little tootsies moving?'

Maggie gritted her teeth and her magic began to build. Her fingers started to tingle and tiny sparks fizzed from her hair.

'Oh, I'm sorry but we have to get going,' said Mum as she took Maggie by the shoulders and quickly steered her to the changing rooms.

Bat climbed out of Maggie's towel and hid in Mum's handbag instead. He had turned bright red again!

CHAPTER 4

Exactly one week later, Mum came rushing into Maggie's room. She was holding a rolled-up towel under one arm and the dreaded duck-covered swimsuit in her other hand.

'Come on, Maggie,' she said, placing the towel and swimsuit onto Maggie's bed. 'It's time for your swimming lesson.'

'But that was last week!' said Maggie.

'It's every week,' said Mum, 'until you learn to swim.'

'But … but … that's SOOOOO unfair!' howled Maggie.

'It's for your own good,'
said Mum. 'Anyway, Bat's
really looking forward to it!'
Bat popped out of Maggie's
towel and nodded his head.

'TRAITOR,'

said Maggie, and Bat ducked
back into the towel again.

At the pool, Bat climbed onto Maggie's swimming cap and turned himself white to match. The cap looked a bit bigger and lumpier than before but nobody seemed to notice.

Mrs Flotsam went over to a giant orange bucket that was full of long, colourful tubes called noodles. 'These will help you to float,' she said as she handed two to each Tadpole.

Maggie put her noodles under
her arms and began bobbing up and
down in the pool. Arthur, however,
couldn't seem to get his noodles in the
right place. He looked as if he were
wrestling with a bright pink octopus.

Maggie could feel Bat shaking as
he tried to hide his giggles.

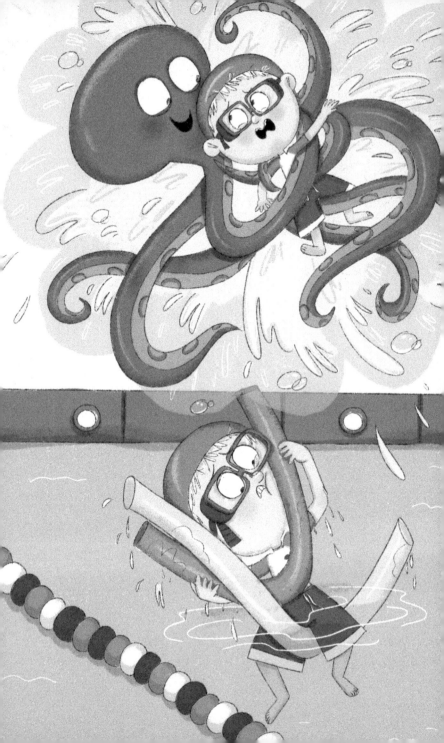

Arthur sighed, pushed the noodles away in disgust and grabbed the side of the pool. 'This is hopeless,' he said. 'I can't float because my legs are too heavy.'

This made Bat laugh even more.

'IT'S NOT FUNNY,' Maggie
told Bat. 'Can you float, Mr Clever
Clogs?'

Bat nodded his head.

'How?' asked Arthur.

Bat started gulping air into
his tummy until he blew up like
a chameleon-shaped balloon.

Then he plopped into the water and bobbed up and down for a bit, before doggy-paddling over to the side of the pool. He climbed out and gave a little bow.

'Show off,' said Maggie as
Bat curled up on her towel and
camouflaged himself to match it.
But Bat had given her an idea. She
could help Arthur float – she just
needed a little bit of MAGIC!

When nobody was looking,
Maggie took her wand out of her
swimming cap, gave it a wiggle and
whispered:

Wind blow foul
and wind blow fair,
pump Arthur Potts
full of air!

POOF!

'WOW!'

said Arthur as his tummy started
to fill with air. 'Hey, look at me,
Maggie. I'm floating ... with no
noodles!'

Arthur's tummy was getting
bigger and bigger and bigger. He
started rising up, out of the pool.

'Oh no!' gasped Maggie. If she
couldn't stop the spell, Arthur
would end up stuck to the ceiling
like an escaped
party balloon.

Then Arthur did a great big

BUUUURP!

His tummy shrank and he plopped back down, so that he was floating perfectly in the water.

Mrs Flotsam turned to look at them. 'Oh, well done, Arthur!' she shouted. 'Since you can float so well, why don't you try swimming?'

Arthur was about to say, 'No, thank you,' when his tummy started making strange noises. URGLE ... GURGLE ... URGLE.

'Oh no!' he said. 'I think I'm going to ...'

PAAAAAAAAAAA

Arthur shot across the water like
a speedboat, leaving a trail of whiffy
bubbles in his wake. He sped all the
way to the other side of the pool.

AAARP!

All the Tadpoles clapped and
cheered and Mrs Flotsam leapt up
and down with excitement. Arthur
looked more surprised than everyone
else and Maggie felt very pleased
with herself.

When the lessons had finally finished, Mrs Flotsam blew her whistle and called all of the classes together at the side of the pool.

'Just before you all go,' she said, 'I wanted to tell you about someone who has done so well today that I'm going to give them the SUPERSTARFISH award!'

'OOOOOHHHH,' went all the children.

Hardly anyone was given the
SUPERSTARFISH award.

'And the award goes to …'
Mrs Flotsam paused
and Ella walked
confidently over to
accept the prize.

'Oh, no, it's not you dear,' Mrs Flotsam told her.

'IT'S ARTHUR POTTS!'

Ella's mouth dropped open. She blushed and scuttled back into the crowd. Everyone clapped and cheered for Arthur, who stood, holding his trophy, with a huge smile on his face.

Maggie was pleased for Arthur, but after ten minutes, she was getting really bored of Mrs Flotsam telling him how *amazing* he was. Then she started telling Maggie that if she tried *really* hard she could be as good as Arthur one day.

Maggie dragged her feet as she walked across the car park, her soggy swimming things slung over her shoulder. Mum was giving Arthur a lift home too, so they all bundled into the car and put on their seatbelts.

'Maggie?' said Arthur.

'WHAT?' snapped Maggie.

'Mrs Flotsam said that because I did so *amazingly* well today …'

Maggie sighed and rolled her eyes. She was beginning to regret using her magic on Arthur.

'... that I could be a Duckling instead of a Tadpole, if I wanted,' Arthur finished.

Maggie gasped. 'And what did you say?'

'I told her that I would rather be a good Tadpole than a rubbish Duckling. So I'll stay and be a Tadpole, with you.'

'Thanks Arthur!' said Maggie. 'You really are my best friend.'

The lovely moment was rather
spoilt when the last of the air
escaped from Arthur's tummy and
they had to open all of the windows.

CHAPTER 5

After trying every excuse she could
imagine, Maggie decided that the
only way she could get out of
swimming lessons
was to learn
to swim.

Week after week she tried, but she just couldn't do it. Arthur, meanwhile, was feeling a lot more confident after winning the SUPERSTARFISH award. He was swimming and splashing and floating, all without the help of Maggie's magic. So were all the other Tadpoles. But Maggie wasn't getting any better.

To make matters worse, Mum
decided to take Alfie to the baby
swimming group, Little Tiddlers.
This meant that they all had to go to
the swimming pool extra early and
Arthur and Maggie had to watch
Alfie's lesson before theirs began.

It was a DISASTER.

Alfie was brilliant! He
splashed in the water.
He charmed all the
other mums (and
Mrs Flotsam).

And by the end of the lesson, he was swimming like an otter cub. It was so unfair!

'Why can everyone swim except me?' Maggie grumbled to herself, after yet another boring lesson in Tadpole class.

While the children were all heading back to the changing rooms, Mrs Flotsam had "a quiet word" with Mum. But it wasn't very quiet at all.

'I'm afraid your Maggie is what I like to call a FOREVER TADPOLE!' she boomed, her voice reaching every corner of the room. 'She really does seem to be a bit of a HOPELESS CASE! But don't worry, I'll give her some one-to-one lessons starting right now. I'm sure we'll make a Duckling out of her, or maybe even a Guppie. But I can't see her EVER being a Shark like her dear cousin Ella.'

Maggie had heard every word … and so had Ella!

'Never mind, Maggie,' Ella whispered, grinning from ear to ear. 'We can't all be Sharks.'

Mum took Alfie to get changed and
soon there was just Mrs Flotsam and a
very grumpy Maggie left in the pool.

'Right, Maggie,' said Mrs Flotsam,
climbing out of the pool and over to
a large cupboard. 'I'll just get you my
special ducky float and before you know

it, you'll be whizzing around the pool like all the other Tadpoles.'

'I don't want to be a Tadpole or a Duckling or a Guppie,' Maggie called after her. 'I want to be a SHARK, like Ella!'

Then Maggie had an idea.

I helped Arthur to swim, she thought, *so maybe I could help myself too. It's time for a little bit of magic!*

Maggie pulled her wand out of her swimming cap, gave it a wiggle and whispered:

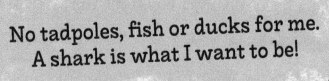

No tadpoles, fish or ducks for me.
A shark is what I want to be!

POOF!

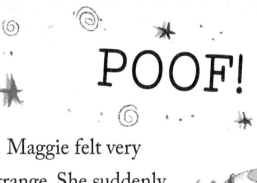

Maggie felt very strange. She suddenly felt a lot bigger than usual. Enormous, even! She wiggled and a triangle-shaped fin popped out of her back. She opened her mouth and her teeth grew into large, sharp points.

Then she tried to wave Mrs Flotsam
over, but her arms and legs had
turned into fins! Oh no! She'd turned
into a REAL SHARK!

Mrs Flotsam turned around, spotted
the shark and fell into the water.
'AAAAAAAAHHHHHHHH!'
she screamed.

She stared at the curly-haired,
freckle-faced shark as it started
swimming towards her.

Maggie had never been underwater
before. It was great! It was cool and quiet
and blue. Well, apart from the water
underneath Mrs Flotsam's legs, which
were thrashing and splashing in panic.

Maggie noticed something shiny on the bottom of the pool and picked it up in her sharp, shark teeth. She was going to show it to Mrs Flotsam, but Mrs Flotsam had clambered out of the water and run off screaming,

'SHARK! THERE'S A SHARK AND I THINK IT'S EATEN MAGGIE!'

Mum came rushing back
to the pool with Alfie in her
arms. She quickly guessed
what had happened. She knew
that there was no time to
waste. The leisure centre staff
would soon come rushing in
and Mum couldn't let them
see Maggie like this. She
popped Alfie into the bucket
full of pool noodles. Then she
fished her wand out of her
handbag, gave it a wave
and chanted:

That's quite enough of naughty sharks.

Change back into Maggie Sparks!

POOF!

The spell worked. Maggie turned back into a little girl again – a little girl who couldn't swim and was underwater in the middle of the swimming pool!

Maggie held her breath and tried to remember what she'd been taught. She moved her arms like a washing machine and kicked her "little tootsies" and, to her surprise, found herself swimming back up to the surface. She kept kicking and splashing until, with a bump, she reached the edge of the pool.

Mum helped Maggie out and gave her a big, rather soggy hug. 'Maggie,' she said, 'what were you thinking?! You can't do magic outside of the house.

Especially not when other people are around!'

'But Mum, didn't you see me?' said Maggie. 'I swam underwater and on the top too!'

'I know you did, and I am so proud but–'

Just then, Mrs Flotsam came running in with a crowd of worried-looking people behind her.

'Look! There's a shark!' she cried.

'Where?' everyone asked.

Maggie and her mum were standing beside an empty pool, and Alfie was busily chewing holes in a noodle.

'B-b-but, it was there, in the water! It chased me. I didn't even have time to blow my whistle,' said Mrs Flotsam, reaching up to grab it. 'My whistle! I've lost my whistle!'

The leisure centre manager put a towel over Mrs Flotsam's shoulders and tried to calm her down. 'Let me make you a nice cup of tea,' she said. 'You've been working much too hard lately. Maybe you could do with a holiday?'

The manager started to lead Mrs Flotsam away when Maggie ran over. 'Mrs Flotsam! I found this at the bottom of the pool,' she said, handing over something silver and shiny.

'My whistle,' gasped Mrs Flotsam. 'Oh, thank you, Maggie! But ... wait a minute, how did you get it from the bottom of the pool?'

'She swam down and fetched it,' said Mum. 'Then she paddled back to the side again. Your one-to-one lesson must have really helped.'

Mrs Flotsam's mouth dropped open. 'That's amazing, Maggie,' she said in a shaky voice.

'Mrs Flotsam,' said Arthur, stepping forwards. 'As Maggie has done SOOOOOOO amazingly well today, don't you think that she deserves the SUPERSTARFISH award?'

'NO!' shouted Ella.

Everyone gasped and looked at Ella, who quickly added, 'No … no one deserves it more!'

'Well said, Ella,' said Mrs Flotsam. 'And yes, you're quite right, Arthur. Ella, dear, could you go and fetch the SUPERSTARFISH award from my office?'

Ella stomped off and returned with the shiny, golden SUPERSTARFISH award. She held it out for Mrs Flotsam who said, 'Could you give it to Maggie, please? And let's all give her a big clap!'

Ella found it very hard to let go of the award as she handed it to Maggie. Her smile was so forced that she looked like someone who was struggling to go to the toilet.

Everybody clapped and cheered.

'I was beginning to think that you might be a Forever Tadpole, Maggie,' said Mrs Flotsam. 'But I think you're well on the way to being a Duckling, or maybe even a Guppie!'

'Who knows,' said Maggie, 'one day I might even be a Shark!'

Then she gave Mrs Flotsam a big smile that was full of very sharp, pointy teeth!

Continue the magic in ...

MAGGIE SPARKS

AND THE

TRUTH
DRAGON